AVAILABLE LIGHT

ALSO BY PHILIP BOOTH

Philip Booth

Available Light

The Viking Press New York

81 1
B

First published in 1976 by The Viking Press, Inc.
625 Madison Avenue, New York, N.Y. 10022

Published simultaneously in Canada by
The Macmillan Company of Canada Limited

Library of Congress Cataloging in Publication Data
Booth, Philip E.
   Available light.

   Poems.
   I. Title.
PS3503.0532A95   811'.5'4   75-38875
ISBN 0-670—14310-3

Printed in U.S.A.

In versions now slightly revised, these poems originally appeared in the following journals:
The American Pen: "Laboratory"; *The American Poetry Review*: "Word"; *The American Scholar*: "Household," "Panic," and "Prides Crossing"; *The Atlantic Monthly*: "Natural History"; *The Antioch Review*: "Landfall"; *Esquire*: "Impotence"; *Field*: "Ways" and "Stations"; *Harper's Magazine*: "Dark," "Self-Portrait," "How to See Deer"; *The Hudson Review*: "Peru"; *Kayak*: "Strata" and "This Dream"; *The Nation*: "Vermont"; *The New Republic*: "Adding It Up," "Dreamscape," "Entry," "How the Blind," and "Old Poem"; *The New Yorker*: "A Late Spring: Eastport," "Stove," and "The Winter of the Separation"; *Poetry*: "A Number of Ways of Looking at It," "Seeing Auden Off," "The Heavy Poet," and "Moment"; *Poetry Northwest*: "A Dream of Russia," "Let the Trees," "Moles," "Photographer," "Wear," and "Native"; *Salmagundi*: "Graffito"; *Shenandoah*: "Longleaf Pine: Georgia" and "Strip"; *The Virginia Quarterly Review*: "Opening Up" and "The Way Tide Comes"; *The Yale Review*: "A Number of Rooms."

Thanks to the editors involved for first printing these poems, and for permission to reprint them. Thanks to Syracuse University for the leave which let me complete this book. Thanks to John Cohen and Edward Ranney (*Aperture* 16:1) for heightening my sense of Peru. To Jay Meek, who read many of these poems in draft, who has asked much of them and has been their most acute critic, thanks most of all.

P.B.

Castine, Maine, 1975

FOR JOANN FINEMAN

CONTENTS

*Being itself comes out of all origins to meet me.
I myself am given to myself. . . . In losing the substance
of my self I sense Nothingness. In being given to
myself I sense the fullness. . . . I can only maintain
my integrity, can prepare, and can remember.*

— KARL JASPERS

All light is available light.   — PAUL STRAND

Sheer cold here.
Four straight days
below zero, the roof
contracting in
small explosions
all night. Now snow:
snow halfway up
the back shed;
more coming all
morning: the sky
drifted, patched
blue, flakes in
large sizes
lazing against
a small sun.
Around here
they call
these days "open
and shut," by
sunset the wind
will veer and
stiffen; tomorrow
will build on
a windblown
crust. Given
this day, none
better, I try
these words to
quicken
the silence: I
break track
across it
to make myself
known.

THE WINTER OF THE SEPARATION

Where I grew up everything snowed:
from inches to feet of silence, falling
out of the ceiling, onto my bed.
When I came down with the chicken pox,
the field was mica under the phone wires
out the bathroom window. There was no shadow,
not any morning, save in the depth
of my bootprints. I was snowed in,
season on season, size six-and-a-half
in my ski boots, out under weighted pines
with my pheasant tracks and the rabbit stains.
Mothers didn't have skis in that ice age,
my father was always away, and there
never was wind where I drifted, up
to my waist in igloos. Once, through small snow,
my mother came out in her own new flurry
to call me home: she held out the back
of a black kid glove to let one crystal settle.
She explained, she tried to explain, all sides.
When her hand barely touched me, I melted.

STOVE

I wake up in the bed my grandmother died in.
November rain. The whole house is cold.
Long stairs, two rooms through to the kitchen:
walls that haven't been painted
in sixty years. They must have shone then:
pale sun, new pumpkin, old pine.

Nothing shines now but the nickel trim
on the grandmother stove, an iron invention
the whole room leans to surround; even
when it is dead the dogs sleep close behind it.
Now they bark out, but let rain return them;
they can smell how the stove is going to be lit.

Small chips of pine from the woodshed. Then
hardwood kindling. I build it all into the firebox,
on top of loose wads of last June's *Bangor News*.
Under the grate, my first match
catches. Flames congregate, the dogs watch,
the stove begins to attend old wisdom.

After the first noisy moments, I listen for Lora;
she cooked all the mornings my grandmother died,
she ruled the whole kitchen the year I was seven:
I can see Boyd Varnum, a post outside the side door;
he's waiting for Lora, up in the front of the house,
to get right change for his winter squash. Lora says

Boyd's got the best winter squash in the village.
When Boyd gets paid, she ties her apron back on
and lets in the eggman. He has a green wagon.
Lora tells him how last night her husband hit her;
she shows him the marks. All her bruised arms
adjust dampers and vents; under the plates where turnips

are coming to boil, she shifts both pies in the oven.
The dogs feel warmer now. I bank on thick coal.

3

The panes steam up as sure as November: rain,
school, a talkative stove to come home to at noon;
and Lora sets my red mittens to dry on the nickel shelves
next to the stovepipe. Lora knitted my mittens.

I can still smell the litter of spaniels
whelped between the stove and the wall; there's
venison cooking, there's milktoast being warmed on
the furthest back plate, milktoast to send upstairs
to my dead mother's mother. Because, Lora says,
she is sick. Lora says she is awful sick. When Lora goes up

to my grandmother's bed, I play with the puppies
under the stove; after they suckle and go back to sleep,
because I am in second grade and am seven, I practice
reading the black iron letters raised on the black oven door;
even though I don't know who Queen Clarion was,
I'm proud I can read what the oven door says: it says

Queen Clarion
Wood & Bishop
Bangor, Maine
1911

This is the pure time.

Nobody but me is awake.
Not in this house. Nobody
anywhere that I know.

But everyone I imagine.

A nurse in mid-shift, over coffee,
telling her probie to keep
a good eye on 514.

A hundred miles due north
of this house, a switchman
shoveling freightyard drifts,

his torch waiting for trains.
The gulls on Jake's Wharf,
still folded in sleep, dreaming

as far as gulls dream: of
the new town dump. One Old Squaw,
a black duck with both eyes open,

already woken in the Back Cove.

I've only begun to see how
I feel, to believe who I am,
to trust what I know.

It's time.

Exactly six months from now,
to the moment, the sun will just
have come up through this window.

MOLES

The rain slants.
Snow compresses.
At this far end
of its steep traverse,
weather sinks in.

Save for two cold
handfuls of leaves,
hung like lost gloves
on an oak's low branch,
the hedgerow is naked.

There's nothing, seen
through this glass
from the in side,
a man might want
to keep in his eye:

nothing not gray,
drenched black, or
wet white. It sticks:
dead-weight limbs jut
into dead pastures.

The wet adds weight
to each stone on
the wall that holds white;
everything's heavy:
nothing weighs more

than the air itself;
it records its own
pressure: a man behind
a window looks out:
he thinks that if

he let his mouth open
a crow would fly
back in. Outside of
his mind the wind
picks up: the junco

riding the oak
takes off. Blind
in translucent blue
caves in old snow,
the moles do not think,

they listen: they hear
wings settle, the barn wind
claw and hammer a plank.
Their season's melting.
They feel how nails sink.

A LATE SPRING: EASTPORT

On the far side
of the storm
window, as close

as a tree
might grow to
a house,

beads of rain
hang cold
on the lilac:

at the tip of
each twig each
bud swells green;

tonight out
there each
branch will be

glazed, each
drop will
freeze solid:

the ice, at
sunrise, will
magnify every

single
bud; by this
time next

week, in-
side this
old glass,

the whole
room will
bloom.

He inhabits weather.
That lemon sun at
his windowshade; he wakes
and dozes, letting the cloudbank
build: light easterlies
all day. Yesterday opened
to thick-of-fog; he checked
his mowed hillside: *cobwebs*
by seven sun by eleven.
By noon it came clear,
sou'west. Come fall
the clearnesses simplify:
raw dawn gusts calming
into a stillness, northwest
easing-off west, the slow
cumulus building tall.
Tomorrow already promises:
a mackerel sky and
the wind backed east;
he can already hear nightrain
on his bedroom roof. He'll wake to
a three-day blow
and he knows it; his gut
is singing low-pressure tunes.
If the radio's on it's on
short-wave weather: Edmonton
gives him winds aloft, he gets
the dew point from Ottawa,
and hears the ceiling in
Syracuse: a whole system
of weather moving his way.
He lives where eaves
drip, his cheek turned
to the slightest windshift,

9

his eye on how sunlight
declines or inclines
to color. The planet spins
winds at him, cold fronts
and equinoctial storms.
He warms himself by rooting
himself in the windswirl; rain
tomorrow, rain for a week:
he couldn't care less.
Or more. There's nowhere
he'd rather be.

Through rain. The fog is in.
The drive's as green as moss.

We let dogs fly; unlatch,
and lean locks open. Where

must was there air must be.
Sashes creak; we undress

sheeted chairs, unroll
the desk, tear calendars,

pick mail, run water clear.
Great-grandfather sits on

the kitchen mantel: we light
damp ashes in his eyes;

they follow every move.
He doubts. How far we've come!

We toast his health. Up stairs
we pour new nightcaps to

the dark. The dark knows dark
in every leaf. The dark

itself is green. We're here:
we've come the long way back.

We make the bed. The dark
turns warm: I'm back to roots,

you feel like moss. Through
fog the rain rains home.

THE WAY TIDE COMES

It came close from out far,
the way tide comes, changing
its levels with such consistent
slowness that—before I
knew it—height became depth,
and where you danced barefoot,

a half-tide ago, covered itself,
under so moving a shimmer
I could not conceive of the weight,
or recall all those shapes
the weight, as it climbed, erased.
We'd kept to old ways, building

a beachfire well above tideline,
ritual at the pure height of summer;
we'd piled driftwood on,
all we could gather. I was
skipping flat stones, you
were trying to keep count; leaning

to throw, I felt distances shift:
it was no longer coming but
like the light of summer itself,
longest the day when summer began,
had already flooded and made
its insistent turn. As once it came

slowly, so now it pulls back
with the quick of evening light:
it will, in due time, uncover
the furthest rocks we swam up on,
even the morning shallows where we
first waded. Tonight's full moon

has already cast off the horizon
it hugely climbed; it's going, before

long, to tug the whole cove empty.
We slept once pretending a larger
knowledge; now we love better.
Let love be; let the heel-and-toe

of your improvised jig, marginal
even at noon, or my sweater,
speared by the branch of a beachlog,
remain our private highwater mark.
There's nothing left, nothing to add,
for which the tide will not account:

fire, our awkward toes where
we yield, the periwinkles' slow track;
no matter how we want, beyond doubt,
to stay the tide or inform it, we
come in time to inform ourselves: we have
to follow it all the way out.

My mind's eye opens before
the light gets up. I
lie awake in the small dark,
figuring payments, or how
to scrape paint; I count
rich women I didn't marry.
I measure bicycle miles
I pedaled last Thursday
to take off weight; I give some
passing thought to the point
that if I hadn't turned poet
I might well be some other
sort of accountant. Before
the sun reports its own weather
my mind is openly at it:
I chart my annual rainfall,
or how I'll plant seed if
I live to be fifty. I look up
words like "bilateral symmetry"
in my mind's dictionary; I consider
the bivalve mollusc, re-pick
last summer's mussels on Condon Point,
preview the next red tide, and
hold my breath: I listen hard
to how my heart valves are doing.
I try not to get going
too early: bladder permitting,
I mean to stay in bed until six;
I think in spirals, building
horizon pyramids, yielding to
no man's flag but my own.
I think a lot of Saul Steinberg:
I play touch football on one leg,
I seesaw on the old cliff, trying

to balance things out: job,
wife, children, myself.
My mind's eye opens before
my body is ready for its
first duty: cleaning up after
an old-maid Bassett in heat.
That, too, I inventory:
the Puritan strain will out,
even at six a.m.; sun or no sun,
I'm Puritan to the bone, down to
the marrow and then some:
if I'm not sorry I worry,
if I can't worry I count.

WEAR

I hate how things wear out.

Not elbows, collars, cuffs;
they fit me, lightly frayed.

Not belts or paint or rust,
not routine maintenance.

On my own hook I cope
with surfaces: with all

that rubs away, flakes off, or fades
on schedule. What eats at me

is what wears from the in-
side out: bearings, couplings,

universal joints, old
differentials, rings,

and points: frictions hidden
in such dark they build

to heat before they come
to light. What gets to me

is how valves wear, the slow
leak in old circuitry,

the hairline fracture under
stress. With all my heart

I hate pumps losing prime,
immeasurable over-

loads, ungauged fatigue
in linkages. I hate

myself for wasting time
on hate: the cost of speed

came with the bill of sale,
the rest was never under

warranty. Five years
ago I turned in every

year; this year I rebuild
rebuilt parts. What hurts

is how blind tired I get.

IMPOTENCE

It won't.

It thinks it wants to.
It wants to think so.
It feels it's too thoughtful.

It lies.

It's scared it might hurt.
It half hopes it may.
It softens the fact that it has.

It can't.

It's big, finally, on self-respect.
It feigns easy sleep.
It dreams hard.

DREAMSCAPE

On the steep road
curving to town, up
through spruce trees
from the filled-in canal,
there have been five houses, always.

But when I sleep
the whole left side of the blacktop
clears itself into good pasture.
There are two old horses,
tethered. And a curving row
of miniature bison, kneeling,

each with his two front hooves
tucked in neatly under the lip
of the asphalt. I am asleep.
I cannot explain it. I do not
want to explain it.

PLANE

We look up at a stutter we used to be tuned to.

Another one run out of sky.

A blunt silhouette,
the long greenhouse, the old
Navy war paint: a Helldiver,
landing gear down,
driven around and around the low sky.

Both hatches back, only one head showing,
the one in the deep back cockpit. He's
standing, almost into the slipstream:
flying suit, goggles, helmet, the works;
he gives his old short-arm salute
to the whole local war.

It goes round again, one
more time, through the sun,
then slides down over a knoll.

The noise empties.

We run and run.

This morning, while I was sleeping,
an unfledged hawk fell out
of the loft overhead. His talons

sank in my neck. I undid
the hooks before breakfast,
blood all over. He

clamped himself onto the bale
of old hay where I tossed him.
His left wing felt broken,

maybe I did it. We
gave each other the eye.
This is the kind of morning

I keep on having: bloody attacks
from every direction.
My woman's got no talent

for nature; never spotted
a grackle, much less a hawk.
When I got down for beer

this morning, she looked up
and down me, and asked, twice,
if maybe I'd cut myself shaving.

On the Trans-Siberian
Railroad, far
east of the Urals, years
before the last war,
the eastbound train
cranked to a stop
in the absolute
middle of nowhere.

We all got out.

It was high summer,
it must have been June,
in that labored cut
through the low
hills, somewhere
west of Omsk; the fields
were full of buttercups.

A conductor, tipping
his cap, came up to tell us
the last car had a hotbox;
the axle of the last truck
was, for a fact, burnt out.
It would take an hour to fix,
perhaps two hours.

The men smoked.
They stood at ease on
the roadbed; the women
climbed up the bank
into pastures.

Somebody in authority
must have telegraphed
ahead, perhaps

to Omsk, or back
to someone he knew
in Moscow.

The men walked back
alongside the track
as they smoked, to inspect
the burnt-out truck.
It had melted all right, the cap-
end of the axle, melted
beyond repair.

We waited under that empty
Russian sky for more
than an hour, while
the hotbox end of the axle
cooled from red hot
to lukewarm. Men spat on it,
or patted it, to tell;
they made bets. But nobody
seemed to doubt that help
would eventually come.

It came, all right! Oh it
came: a blur
becoming four men, rolling
in front of them—up
the long track behind us—
a widening great steel axle,
a new axle and two new wheels, welded
as one.

While we cheered them on,
and the trainwhistle blew
from the engine end, the women
returned to the top of the cut,
standing with hiked-up skirts against
the near horizon,
humming some Russian song.

Then the conductor
directed the men,
perhaps a hundred men,

to lift
the last car.

They heaved and did it,
swearing a great
conglomerate oath,
as though they were moving
heaven and earth.

He held them there for
the crucial minute,
conducting in that same dialect
he must have sent
by telegraph. And while
they held, new men
moved out the old axle;
and those four men
from somewhere back toward the Urals
rolled in the new one. Then
the conductor gave
a signal; they let down easy, and
there she was.

All this was years
before the last war, somewhere
east of the Urals.
I tell you that trainwhistle blew
while the men climbed back aboard
and we got ready to start toward
the east again
on the Trans-Siberian
Railroad: east toward
Omsk and Lake Chany and
in another week,
Vladivostok.

It had taken exactly two hours.

Oh, when that whistle blew
the women came down from
the railroad bank
and the long pastures
behind them; they pelted

the axle-pushers with skirts full
of buttercups, of what looked like
daisies, and with wild hundreds
and hundreds of wild Russian
flowers.

We are men, ranked on stainless stools, each swung out
from under a stainless bench. Each of us holds,
in his left hand, a gum-rubber tube. Into the end
of the tube, with each right hand, we shoot
a small hypodermic needle. We think there are people
below us, over the far sharp edge of the bench,
people injected when we flood the needle.
We never see them. We never have. Whenever one of us
feels like looking, he pulls the steel handle
over his head. Save for the man who pulls,
every stool except his, along the whole row, flips up
and over, and plunges; everybody who isn't him
becomes, almost instantly, them.

LANDFALL

Dreaming, offshore,
the low green mound of an island
I was about to land on,

I wake to dip
in a deep blue cup of a pond,
set in steep hills, far inland.

THIS DREAM

I climb up from this dream
the way, last fall, I finally
survived diving into a quarry:
by swimming, from dark, for
light as hard as pink granite.
They tell me I almost drowned.
Warm as I've grown, I'm
of no mind to remember.
As if from deep cold, I only know
to invite myself back: I tip
my eyes empty of sleep; then,
with the heel of each hand, I tap
the ringing out of each temple.
The small bells keep on.
If this is fever, I want it.
Everything's clear: the sun
has come back from nowhere,
and brought with it incalculable light.
This morning will not go away.
No more will I: I am in my element;
I baptize myself by breathing my name,
I give my new face to the sun.
I smile like everything, even
at me: I think I am perfectly mad:
I believe I will live forever.

I hunt.
I hunt light.
Not easy noon.
Not mere sun.
But how shadows winnow:
the early moment,
the dignity that grows late.

Wherever I learn to see
I turn native. The trees tell me.
I give thanks to lichen.
I sit against rocks to reflect.

I remember my fathers: the game
they sought. The track, sight,
and spear, the caves they came back to:
the tall walls they wrote on,
graced by low light.

Shapes, pulsing!

The brave stillness.

Old light and new light
pivot and climb; there's nowhere now
for a man's eye to sleep.
I hunt far in, as deep as
light moves; where light steeps
in the long momentum.

Not that it holds, it
changes. The changes
balance. Before they tip through
to regroup I let

my eye open, fill
for a fraction of
truth, and shut:
                    I keep for life
how light
shapes how
lives deepen.

Forget roadside crossings.
Go nowhere with guns.
Go elsewhere your own way,

lonely and wanting. Or
stay and be early:
next to deep woods

inhabit old orchards.
All clearings promise.
Sunrise is good,

and fog before sun.
Expect nothing always;
find your luck slowly.

Wait out the windfall.
Take your good time
to learn to read ferns;

make like a turtle:
downhill toward slow water.
Instructed by heron,

drink the pure silence.
Be compassed by wind.
If you quiver like aspen

trust your quick nature:
let your ear teach you
which way to listen.

You've come to assume
protective color; now
colors reform to

new shapes in your eye.
You've learned by now
to wait without waiting;

as if it were dusk
look into light falling:
in deep relief

things even out. Be
careless of nothing. See
what you see.

Not fog but cloud
gusts onto the mule walled in
with one thin tree
in this stone farmyard.

The tree bends like an Inca's longbow:
the wind is climbing the side of the Andes.

The mule lies folded against the old wind,
his ears peaked like
the small thatched mountain that comes
and goes
through the cloud: a stone barn
held together by mud. Thatch, mud, stone;
the mule knows how they feel.

He almost sleeps, almost content: miles
behind his eyes, at rest for this moment
against the tall winds of Peru, he
dreams the perfect burden of granite,

granite his ancestors carried,
hundreds of years ahead
of him, up
from Pisac, to form
in Machu Picchu the white steps built to
the highest shrine: the *hitching-
post-of-the-sun.*

Down steep generations,
thatch, mud, stone, hold their own like
white granite. Under the wind-
struck cloud of a darker solstice,
his eyes closed on winter, the mule
does not need to look. His blood believes.
He can already hear the sun come
galloping back.

LONGLEAF PINE: GEORGIA

Immersed
in papery
slabs of
bark, their
ends lightly
adrift,
        his eye
climbs back
the anchored
trunk, up
to twenty
times as
deep as
a man;
        his eye
sways, dizzy
before the
first branch
floats, its
quick needles
and pitched
cones buoyed
to surface
in sun.
        His eye
heightens: to
meet the black-
bird fishing
from pine to
pine, its
shadow dark
in the waving
shadows that,
at the bottom,

can drown
a man;
      his eye,
unwilling to
sink, swims
up from
dark, back
up through
pinetop under-
growth: grown
still as
Georgia
under its
millpond
sky.

STRATA

after Gary Snyder's first line

The desk is under the pencil.
Under the desk
the floor, under the floor
old earth itself.

The poem is under the words.
Over the words
the pencil; the mind, above
all, hovers.

Erase the pencil, floor
the desk; allow
the mind be grounded. Never
surfaces, only

strata: pacific, far
offshore, sounding
to feed, lunging to breathe,
the great gray whales

—almost extinct—still
migrate. They move
by instinct under Pegasus,
under Pisces,

and Cetus: over the skeleton-
crews of drowned bombers,
who cannot speak
for the planet.

Let the trees be full.
                Full,
you ask, for God's sake of *what?*
Leaves in due season, or snow;
a moon, if it comes to that.
Or, lacking as much, a night
after clouds full of wind.
                    What
do you mean you don't know
what I mean? Get out
of the house and into
the trees. You, through
fall-out and smoke, who
for six gravid days
have program'd yourselves
into space, tracking
your progress through
wavelengths converged
on hundreds of lenses. . . .

It's no great matter what
starlings have already
flown, or stiffly still wait
in the branches; the seeds,
from their warm apogee,
have spun toward hard
re-entry. Refusing
how winter answers
your doubt, you might
even want, toward new
growth, to kneel at the root
of what you look up at.

Look, I say, to the trees,
and let your two eyes

fill them, even as then
your own two eyes may
be filled.
            We've looked
long enough at ourselves:
for six brave days without
love, computing cold pride
through a hundred lenses.
Proud of voyage less than
return, we've left no
hero in space; nor is
there a tree on the moon,
to feast on or look up to.

The computers whirr and blaze
in their own trajectory,
plotting how men return
to Texas to tell their story
to punchcards. Conditioned
to die, we watch ourselves
orbit on padded couches, banking
on tapes to program our
last defenses.
            Look
out the window, you
who have planted a tree
in your yard, or live
on the edge of a hedgerow;
you, whom computers have
fired, and gravity finally
tugged home: I pray you,
come to your senses.

That narrow sea.
A hard riptide.
The waves take centuries
to break.

A NUMBER OF ROOMS

WALKER EVANS, 1904–1975

A small black room.
An intricate door.

It opens and shuts
according to numbers.

The back wall is silver.
Light enters the archive

for instants of life:
Pacific driftwood,

the immigrant steerage,
a mare at full gallop,

snow in New York;
a burnt Chinese baby;

Baudelaire, a white picket.
The back wall is silver:

the back wall remembers.
The back wall remembers

two open doorways in
Enfield, New Hampshire:

a parlor doorway past
a stilled rocker, down

the negative dining-
room, into a kitchen

through a second door:
from light through dark

back to light: the ceiling's
acoustic-tile squares.

Through a seven-element-
lens, what one eye held

in three Enfield rooms
is, beyond their tilt floor,

the sharp balance of
cold new controls,

controls exposed with-
out comment: the therm-

ostat, lightswitches,
mail-order switch-

plates and plastic
fixtures, ex-

posed and mounted on
plain country walls.

A NUMBER OF WAYS OF LOOKING AT IT

I

In farms along the Savannah,
in Davenport apartments,
in Spokane hotels, people

wake to it on their own time,
by dawn's first wintry light.
Sometimes the flag is up

already; sometimes it plays
a difficult anthem, or starts
the morning with an old name.

It has been on all night in
a room in downtown Washington:
a lidless eye heavy with snow.

II

When it's today
at least three people
announce that it is.

When it's tonight
it only takes two
to tell you to
put out the light.

III

It was possible to imagine.
Now that it's here, it's
impossible to contemplate.

IV

It shows more than it tells.
It sells more than it shows.
It best of all shows
how the pros do it:

Check: how to bake French.
Check: how to love Danish.
Check: how to kick Hungarian.

Also: to vote
        the straight
        ticket.

It likes being All-American.

V

When it was little
it used to be big;
now that it's big
it seems small.

It is not an idiot.
I, who account
for it, am not.
It has not yet
sampled me; it
counts me as part
of the broad projection:

executives dream,
in prime time,
of feeding me
into a slot.

VI

It is like a river in which
there were once three channels.

43

Even in both Dakotas, now
those three channels are one.

In South Dakota
the river is moving,

in North Dakota the power
must be back on.

VII

It's exceptional
at big figures,
at close-up
faces, party
games, place
names, races,
and big league
sports. At war
it's largely
professional.

VIII

Dogs can't see it.

IX

Committees invite
advice about it, it
keeps high places awake.

It's how the capitol
looks from Presque Isle,
and how New York sees Bismarck.

X

People on it
most show themselves

when their voices
are fully turned off.

It takes an explicit position
based on an implicit
proposition: life
may be like that.

XI

It's easy to see
it's hard to keep watch:

over breakfast the cities
officially glitter;

the trees in small towns
are dark with snipers,

the roadsides are raw
with steel cleats.

All day long, in spite
of good men, positions

harden, old armor
is backed by new weapons.

This is the program:
private citizens

turned to
platoons of captains;

families torn, canned
speeches, burnt skin.

The advertisements invite
enlistment: people

look up to them,
drinking. The rest

is a serial ordeal:
if one can bear, after

supper, to keep
his eyes open,

the women come on.
The wept-out children,

if you yourself last,
get to you just

before sleep.

SNAPSHOTS FROM KENTUCKY

RALPH EUGENE MEATYARD, 1925–1972

Lots has happened. Especially to barns,
and them who lived behind them.
When the leaves come off

the bare trees quake
all over the place. The kid
looking out from the walnut trunk

is named Meatyard. He's
Lucybelle Crater's sister's
dumb brother. There's other

people, leaning against things,
or sitting in shadows
with masks on. If they don't

have masks on they might
have eyes. A rock might settle
right on their stomach.

They almost get mashed
but they don't: they keep
their selves moving, moving

their selves next to doors
and out windows. They don't want to
end up next to the man

who got two meathooks for one
of his hands. Lots of it blurs
when you try to remember:

like telephone poles
people get staggered by how
weedy the falls grow,

and how who you were
in the park
when they took your picture

47

moved; stuff that's alive
has different speeds
of dying: some grows still,

some don't. If you get
to think about how sills rot,
or about washed mortar letting

bricks float through
the orchard, you might
think gravity don't

exactly hold. Not, any-
ways, here. It's so
things got loose; nothing's

stayed. Nothing and children.
But that don't mean different
than what you see, just

this is the shape
we each was in
when it happened.

THE INCREDIBLE YACHTS

The incredible yachts: stays
and halyards geared to tension,
banks of winches on deck;
they blew into harbor
this evening: richly cruised men
wed to aluminum hulls
and fleet women: they raced
to get here. Once at anchor
in this stormed harbor,
in this indelible weather,
they bobbled the tide with
their empties: none of them
cared to know in truth
what harbor they were in.

Born to Prides Crossing,
privately tutored; finished

at Foxcroft, engaged to
Groton and Harvard, wed

after the Coral Sea
and Midway; bride

to Treasury, wife
to Wall Street and mother

to Gracie Square, she
has been first mate

on three Bermuda races,
and is newly mistress

of one round-the-world
teak ketch. Aboard,

at her grandfather's
inlaid desk, far in

the Caribbean, she
times to her forty-

sixth birthday
her annual letter

to her last tutor.
Her hand is impeccably

North Shore italic:
Since Arthur's corporate

interests require him
to be in Aruba one day

and North of the Arctic
Circle the next, we

live somewhat separate
lives. Whit has been

asked to depart St. Paul's,
after drugs; we don't know

where he goes next. Jilly,
whom you last saw

the summer she was about
to start Chapin,

I have just now flown back
to New York to abort.

I have been hospitalized
myself, but am out

again for a third try.
At least I refuse

what my friends still
in Boston seem nowadays

to feast on: the sacrilege
of an easy Jesus.

Please do not
send me condolences;

I know you will not.
Her script slants

increasingly small: *I sit*
to write you aboard

an anchored sailboat, with my
own name on her transom.

She is perfectly furled. I
am afloat, the crew is ashore;

every halyard and sheet
is perfectly coiled. I sit

wondering, now, if life
will ever unbraid

itself. Or do
I mean unsnarl

51

*itself? I know that you
cannot tell me this. . . .*

*But how, if it does,
will I know that it has?*

This sad house.
Two girls gone.
The third girl

left, fifteen.
Three years to
go. Late from

staying after
school, she eats
alone with both

the same old
parents. Same
old meal: they

drink, she eats;
they eat, she
clears her plate.

Lead questions.
Moral mouth-
fuls. Between

them she grows
old, she tells
the same old

lies. Her sisters
have abandoned
her; she's wiser

than an only
child. She chokes
on what they

all three know,
meal after
meal: the house

is sad, it
cannot
hold.

It is to be out
of familiar walls
with no place left
but the Halfway
House far up
the block: it is,
this first after-
noon, to carefully
ask your new self
for a walk beyond
the drugstore around
the block, but then
to have to refuse;
it is to remember
how trees grow out
of the sidewalk, to
figure how this time
to face him: the one
with hair like old vines,
who steps out of
nowhere, trying to
take you over, back
where he always
comes from; it is
having moved here
instead: here to
sleep, to learn
to get up: it is,
at supper the always
first night, to
try to ask for
the salt. And having it
passed, it's to weep.

LIKE A WOMAN

Like a woman
I loved, I say
words to the dark,
not to suffer.
Grown as I am,
I'm far from
immune: if I'm
in for it long
I want mind to
hold on, words in
my throat ready
to name it. Let
me keep fury
to stay against
pain; if it
is given me
to learn I mean
to know it all
the way, to bear
it like a woman.

IT IS BEING

*. . . the resolution of the will-to-being
to detach itself from all determinate
knowledge of being . . .*
— KARL JASPERS

It is being offshore: nothing that's not horizon.
It is, beyond beacons, sailing alone.
Nothing, beyond one's compass, to point or warn.

It is, as necessity, knowing the old names for stars
blanked by cloud. To home on them is,
as it's given, to steer a singular course:

it is to navigate knowing that no port is home.
It is to assign one's self to the helm;
it is, offshore, repeating for sanity one's own name,

on watch beyond relief. It is standing watch
beyond hope of relief, weathering the blind fetch
of one's heart, and the crabbed set of one's mind.

It is tacking in fog. It is, of a stillness,
to fish with deep hooks. And, if they catch, to bless
with strange names from the masthead all you release.

Where there is nothing that's not horizon
it is, to ease thirst, sucking a fishbone.
It is being outside one's limits, the horizon's one man.

Close to the road east of Machias,
a glass box under a telephone pole,
for miles of dark the one light left on.

Late, walked in out of rain,
a man in a blaze vest folds the door shut,
dials 0, and talks. The box inside

the glass box swallows his dime.
He dials again, pays again, listens,
and quits. Whatever it was he was after

the other end didn't come close.
The rain blows off; the light
stays on, precisely cast. Hooked

back up, the phone starts ringing.
The glass box vibrates, over and
over, then stops. Again, and

again it comes to nothing.
Hundreds of miles of dark.
The man walks back where he came from.

Ithaca last night, Syracuse at noon, Cedar Rapids tonight.
His face cracked like a dry salt flat, a line for every poem,
he tries two airport Gibsons, reserved (behind dark glasses)
for his flight. Sleet primes the runways, candlelight
preserves the bar. The jets suck air, burning their own feces.
Jakarta, Shannon, Idlewild, are everywhere the same.
Ithaca and Syracuse behind him, Iowa tonight.

He autographs deserted landing strips. In Iowa tonight
he'll sign five gins, whet his faults, and lust for limestone.
He has his autopilot on; who am I to name the pieces
into which a poet cracks? *Fire and sleet and candlelight.*
I gulp the beer he pays for, and see through his smeared glasses
the dark impossibility of home. We drink the price of being done
with Ithaca and Syracuse; I wave him off, toward Iowa, tonight.

THE HEAVY POET

> *This is what one does, what one becomes*
> *Because one is afraid to be alone,*
> *Each with his own death in the lonely room.*
> — DELMORE SCHWARTZ

Bunged-up like any general
of Plato's legion, his tongue smoked
with morning shots, the heavy poet
wakes blurred in a new motel.

He dresses himself, still dogged
by creditors, forgetting to zip;
the girl gone from his naked bed,
and no number to dial for help.

Breakfast is now being served.
He eats at his own last poem,
unsure if it's summer, or time
for summer, if that's what he loved.

The clock travails and spills; those birds
like fireworks he once heard burble
explode in his bed's mirror. He reads
his shadow sliding down the wall.

Cane or no
cane, nothing
left or right

to tap, here at
the steep curb,
how the blind

bear themselves:
standing from
the neck down

plumb as granite;
how, in sheer
necessity they

stand, their
bearings
lost, out

of every
depth save
courage,

perspective
unavail-
able, not

knowing who
is near them:
how we

wait for
some foreknown
inflection or

a stranger's
arm, for
someone, anyone

God knows, any
one
to steer them.

STATIONS

The old, their big shoulders humped,
empty grain sacks under each eye,
sit without talk in the waiting room.
In weekly for shots, I've learned to
tell them apart: the doctors who wear
white jackets, old women in discount
dresses, the men with dark pants on.

I guess they must all be dead now:
the Negroes I used to watch back in '44,
each one safe between oak armrests in
an oak pew, waiting for trains or
relatives to arrive, or maybe the war
to end, the far side of the Macon station.

Gratefully,
with family around;
held to known hands:
the old way.

*

In a motel bathroom,
unable to get to
the phone.

*

While sirens flash,
watching blood channel;
trapped in the bite
of acetylene torches.

*

Fog and a mountain:
the warning lights pulse.
A belt in the gut.
All of you.

*

Feeling for handholds
on a sheer face,
cheek to cold stone.

*

The pain,
weighing tons,
shifting.

*

In prison,
the end of a sentence.

*

A red flannel shirt,
jogging, against
traffic.

*

Running uphill
through old films,
under orders.
*
Hearing the whistle
that notes
a trajectory.
*
Tubes at both ends;
paying for it.
Not even the nurses
can smile.
*
Cells eating cells:
childish arithmetic
followed by zeros.
Strangers: counting.
Relatives: counting.
Strangers and relatives,
counting. And counting.
*
Drunk, a half hour before sunrise.
Unable, for once, not
to reach for the gun.
*
Still listening for music.
A band at the corner:
turning maybe this way.
Or that.
*
Barely come out
of your doctor's brick office:
*
counting, already,
how friends will figure.
*
Figuring, newly,
the ways old friends managed.
*
Managing courage:
weeks of more tests.

In a flat month
in a low field

I hit on a word
with just one

meaning. One.
It got to me,

hard. I stood
back up, grabbing

for balance; I
tried to hit

back. But it
meant it: no

matter what I
did nothing

would yield.
I tried old

levers: hope,
belief, love.

Earth would not
give, not for

the world. Not
one prospect

of any appeal.
That was final:

the word itself
would have the last

word; no way
around it, over,

or through. No
reason behind it.

Who, in God's name,
had what in mind?

I dug as deep as
my heart could stand.

OLD POEM

The train you took has taken all night.
East and North now, you wake to fog.
At the last platform a pick-up's waiting.

A kid drives, with headlights on,
focused down close against the blacktop.
No lights come out of the dark to meet you.

Maybe an hour: the road ends steep
on a wharf soft with fog. The fog is tidal:
an oak shows up, its bare limbs dripping.

A luncheonette trailer is parked on the wharf.
The fat woman offers you welcome coffee:
she slides back her window and slides out

the cup. She won't take your money;
she seems to imagine some family resemblance.
Or maybe she's sorry about your old limp.

Her nose is in the wrong part of her face.
She breathes like a foghorn. Her teeth
are as stained as your ebbed mug of coffee.

You, she says, you probably feel
like you just got to The Jumping-Off Place.
Just about then the fog gives up.

The oak stops dripping. The kid backs down,
to hitch his pick-up up to the trailer.
The lunch window locks. There's almost sun.

Now you can see both of the islands:
not far apart, but far miles out.
They look like stains on the pewter ocean.

Save for the islands there's no horizon,
except between them there isn't a seam.
Not even a line between sky and water.

The fisherman down on the float says nothing.
He lets you cast off the boat yourself,
the boat you bought from an ad, sight unseen.

You find she mostly fires on all four.
She only skips sometimes. It doesn't matter.
The islands are straight down the bay,

straight out. There isn't a buoy in sight, or
a ledge. There's no sign of wind, no
other boat. Only the islands over your bow.

There isn't a seam, except between them.
The closer you head the clearer it comes.
What looked from land like old water, old sky,

between the islands divides to new color:
it looks now more like old tin and old lead:
the edge it took half your life to discover,
the edge you've figured all night to get over.

March: a porcupine spent
March nights gnawing sap
from the blue spruce trunk;

he climbed two-thirds of
the cold March branches
before he bit into the bark.

A tree as tall as a house.
Now, midsummer, the sprucegum
still bleeds; like a root

cut quick by the blade
of a mower, the whole upper trunk
slowly gums up.

The porcupine trespasses
still, waddling toward evening
across the backyard like

a dirty quilled panda.
The two dogs might smile,
if they could. They hold back,

from experience. The porcupine,
fat as a garbage pail,
admits, to his nocturnal

seasons, no moral.
The spruce, through July,
dies without sorrow.

My father, 79,
died in his home bed
with no last word,
his jawbone frozen open.

Before the service
while the chimes said
nothing, I—afraid I
might die the same way—

ran to a mens' room
deep in the chapel.
Letting go, I read
pencil on marble:

Time is nature's way
of preventing
everything
from happening all at once.

Father, forgive
my unforgiving mouth:
I sang how those words sang,
I felt the whole stall dance.

WATCH

The hand keeps sweeping across
its seconds; after a minute

the minute changes, number
on number the new hours fall.

Our Roman numerals
glow in the dark

like initials carved
in space. Now and again,

near dawn, we admit to
the domed house we live in:

we allow enough of ourselves
to deny we've been proofed

against tears, or built
resistant to shock.

There is no end to the lies
we devise to live by,

or the limits we claim to die for.
When our bodies fail

we claim the clear glass
of our souls is immortal,

we name ourselves
as deserving heirs,

we light small candles
and wish. Or promise.

Better we name, in true order,
commanders deceased overseas

in the Punic Wars; better,
before old tides and new,

we for once try silence,
love starlight, believe

in morning, and come in our fields
to lean on the morning wind.

Möbius knew: he
figured it out:

this complex plane
does not, by

any equation,
add up to

zero.
It happens barely:

after the turn,
opposites start

to connect,
the event

becomes an act
of relief:

a continuous
map of how, in

half-turning,
a man

can surface to
change; he thumbs

his way home
the long way

around, from
where he is

to where he
intends: he

finds himself
turning

back into
himself.

SELF-PORTRAIT

I am the man who sawed these logs.
I am the man who lugged these logs,
the man who bedded them, one at a time,
between two trees in a hardwood grove.

I am the man who focused on light,
I am the man whose hand got cold;
mine was the eye that saw through fog
to contrasts timed to lighten a wall.

I am a man who ought to be writing.
Words are my trade. I ought to be at it:
every tree in the fog has a name.
But dark or darker? What does light mean?

I am the man who bought a dark house.
I am the man who sealed light from a room.
I think in the dark how little I know.
Who can I tell how quiet I feel?

I am a man who knows he owns woods;
the same man, still, who keeps looking for words.
The logs between trees in the grove are the poem.
I mean nothing except what I love.

MOMENT

The old sting.   Dead.
The bee.   Honey
here on the tongue.

Moment on moment
each moment blooms.
The moment flowers
whether or not
we want it, whether
or not we let it
occur to us.
Nothing happens,
still, without
our knowing. We think,
but what matter?
Once the moment
is over its wild
persistence goes
to seed. Once
and once, over
and over, the present
gives itself up:
the past cannot
remember the future
does not yet know.

The dead sting.   A be-
coming other.   Now.
Here on the tongue.

I

A far coast.
The dark come down early.
Down over the hill, the harbor.
The old heaved sidewalk. By nine
not even a houselight still on.

Under the one corner streetlight
two new figures: they stand strange.
And now another. No car, out of nowhere.
Then here, this corner.

We talk.
          Strange
so familiar: after
a funeral in Halifax once.
It's true. I even imagine
I know the third one.

The draggers start bunting the spiles,
the tide must have turned.

We go down in the dark to see.

Against the pull of the ebb
there are fish who sound small,
flipping the surface.
                    Fish
after fish.
          We listen,
watching the dark.
As if it weren't winter
we swing legs over
the edge of the wharf.

The scallop season opens
at midnight, the men already collecting
under the single light.

What a life.

We haul each other back up.

II

What a life.

Seasons of leaves, interstices
of pure light. Holy days:
solstice and equinox; cold
coming clear and tipping
the balance. We grow
to be old.

The store, the mail, stopping
for gas; mornings of evening
invitations.
     Everyone lives
as though no one knew.

III

Driven home late:
          same old Chevy, same
kid-argument.
          High on headlights, a deer
settles it: sprung almost across the road
in one leap.
       Almost.
       The curve,
the centrifugal pull of a sixpack.

         The power line arcs.
All down the line
all the lights
go out.
       Or a dog, the next noon,

                    in a first spit
of snow. He goes
for the joy of it, running
the wind.   Then, when it
stops, the wind of quick cars. Car
after car.
              Then a gull,
headed crosswind.
                   The driver gets out
and walks back.
                   The blood of the world
floods the dog's mouth.

                        People who know better
cruise after church,
                      spotting the sites;
close to bared apples, they stop
by the Grange where deer browse.
                        Four days to wait,
                        a short season
this year: headlights at dusk
flick down the woods-roads. Guns
racked against the backwindow
of pick-ups.
              Back in the store
the men talk of bearscat.

IV

His wife and son left, a boy
in a loft far inland sleeping off
grief.
          Mice. Winter squash.

He gets up in the cold to do *t'ai chi.*
The first time since July.
Everything in him quivers.

I am learning to be quiet, to listen,
to balance, to try for the balance of us all
whether to continue or to cease.

Behind him the wind clear-cuts the hillside.

Leaves at his feet, the ground frozen,
he stretches, feels his muscles remember each other,
balances, holds, and eases.

I ask myself now as I look at these I's
if there is something to be said
past the realization that there is nothing
to be said.

Parsnips, turnips, hard squash, the root
shapes. A whole spring catalogue
come to bear on the floor of the loft.
They weigh, grown to nightmare.

It is cold in the loft, and when
I do sleep it is sound.

Beyond sleep, in the hardwood valley
where deer in their season
will finally come down,

a hundred Presidents hang racked
on a single tree, each
like a small boy's school-window moon.

I think of the places
we loved. The shore, tides,
the years.
            Moved, they've
gone far. Moved, the boy
writes his letter

much love
            and walks all the way
into Conway to mail it.
                        Miles
of valley carved by the river,
whole geologic ages.
                        Old foothills.
He feels them close:
                millions
of rains on the ridges.

V

The first hard freeze, three calm nights without let-up.
This third morning, black ice:
                              the surface
flowered with frost, the whole marsh frozen into
a stillness:
              the windless channels give way
to islands of marshgrass, bleached ninetails;
                                          the reaches
edge behind larch to maple; beyond their silver,
whole horizons of fir.
                        We sit on mittens,
lacing old skates.
                    I watch you happen to smile,
wondering how we ever came
                            to love.
Next to the outlet, a big pipe under a country road,
the black ice skims to nothing;
                                wondering where
the source is, we skate a surface
                                  barely safe:
the new ice sinks and swells as it takes up
our weight;
              reports crack ahead of us,
blazing our passage, mapping it.
                                  We skate to a drum
we half create, run out of wind
                                and stop, still.
The sky's brittle.
                    Airbubbles pumped out of nowhere
freeze under our feet in mid-ice:
                                  schools of loosed stars,
small planets,
                and moons come to nought.
Surveyors of space
                    new to us, we focus down
through galaxies
                  to eelgrass waving in soft currents;
beetles small as a dot

                         swim at large under
the planets.

We slide a foot toward what an old man wrote
the week before he died:
we live, we have
                    to live, on
                              insufficient
evidence.

It's true: brightly stilted, surfaced on dense shallows,
we steady each other by
                         studying a slow green dance:
newts and frogs
                    tunneled into the silt,
maybe with crayfish and perch
                              covered by last summer's layers:
planaria, husks of dragonflies.
                         Through the ice,
darkly, we half see
                    how the heron lives; frozen out,
the ducks and he
                    took off for God knows where.
The chickadee in the hackmatack whistles his calling across
the marsh, a small solace
                         where we skate
                              filled
with an absence.
                    Who knows what we did to help? Who
                    knows, ever, how to give what's due?
It's true:
          we never know
                    a life
                         enough. . . .

The black ice cracks and holds:
you pump off hard
to the beaver house
                    your far eye just discovered.

Now you shout back
                    through first thin snow
what only the beaver
can hear, or only
the pickerel and hornpout
                    nosed into mud,
or the painted turtle we'll come back to count
                              next spring.
Close to the source
                    I ease across flexible ice
to catch you:
                    opening ourselves
                    between ninetails and snow
                         we come close
                              and hug:
                                   lives
we barely know, lives
                    we keep wanting
to know.